HIPPO RIDES A BIKE

Written by Sue Graves

Illustrated by Trevor Dunton

W

FRANKLIN WATTS

LONDON • SYDNEY

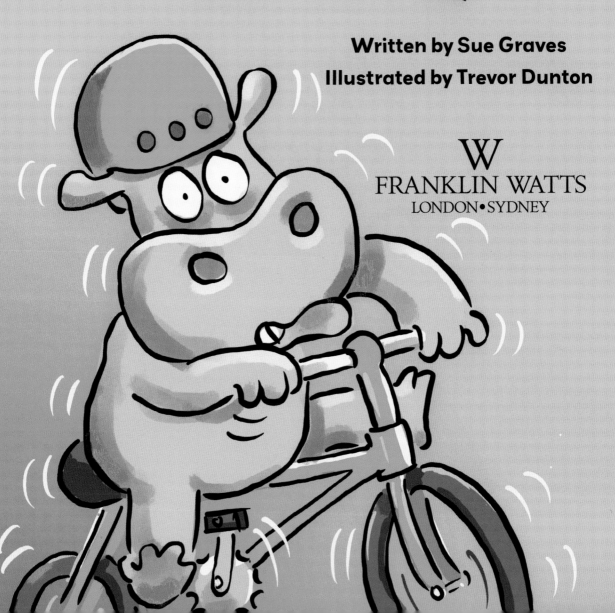

One day, Aunty Hippo gave Hippo a **new bike**. It was big and blue and very shiny! She gave him a new bike helmet, too. Aunty Hippo said it was important to always **wear a helmet** on a bike to keep safe.

Hippo was excited. He wanted to ride his bike **straight away**. He said he wanted to go on a bike ride with his friends.

But Aunty Hippo said Hippo had to **learn** how to ride a bike first. Hippo said he didn't need to learn. He said he could already ride his old trike. He said he would be able to ride a bike easily.

Hippo got on the bike. But he couldn't **keep his balance**. He couldn't turn the pedals. He fell off!

Hippo was cross. He said the bike didn't work properly. He said he didn't want to ride it at all.

Aunty Hippo said he **shouldn't give up**.
She said it took time to learn how to ride a bike.
He had to learn how to balance on it first.
Hippo said he was good at balancing. He said
he could balance on anything.

He said he could even balance on one leg.
He showed her! But Aunty Hippo said balancing
on a bike took **lots of practice**. Hippo was
disappointed.

Then Aunty Hippo told him that when she was a little hippo, she wanted to ice skate. At first, she **couldn't balance** on the skates. But she didn't give up. She **kept trying** and trying and trying.

At last, she could skate. She was very pleased.
Hippo had a think. He said he could keep trying
to ride his bike. Aunty Hippo said that was a very
good idea.

Aunty Hippo held the bike while Hippo got on. He tried to keep his balance. First, he **wobbled** one way. Then he wobbled the other way.

He didn't feel safe at all. But he **didn't give up** and soon Hippo felt much safer.

Then Aunty Hippo said he had to push the pedals
round and round with his feet.

Hippo **tried hard**, but his feet kept missing the pedals. He kept falling off. He was upset.

Then Hippo remembered what his aunty said. He told himself **not to give up**. He got back on the bike.

Hippo pushed on the pedals. He **tried hard**. He wobbled into a large puddle. He got very wet. But he didn't give up.

Hippo tried again. He got on his bike. He tried **really hard**. He wobbled into a hedge.

The hedge was very prickly.

But Hippo didn't give up.

Hippo got back on his bike. He tried **really, really hard**. He pushed on the pedals. He wobbled … and he wobbled.

But Hippo kept going. Soon he was riding his bike really well!
Aunty Hippo said he was brilliant for not giving up. Hippo **was proud**.

The next day, Hippo met up with his friends. He showed them his new bike. His friends said his bike was **amazing**. Then they all went for a bike ride. Hippo said riding a bike was the **best fun ever**!

A note about sharing this book

The *Experiences Matter* series has been developed to provide a starting point for further discussion on how children might deal with new experiences. It provides opportunities to explore ways of developing coping strategies as they face new challenges.
The series is set in the jungle with animal characters reflecting typical behaviour traits and attitudes often seen in young children.

Hippo Rides a Bike

This story looks particularly at a skill that many children find difficult to acquire: riding a bike. It looks at the importance of trying hard and not giving up. It provides a base for examining other skills the children may have found hard and strategies they used to overcome their difficulties. The book also highlights the importance of wearing a helmet when riding a bike.

How to use the book

The book is designed for adults to share with either an individual child, or a group of children, and as a starting point for discussion.
The book also provides visual support and repeated words and phrases to build reading confidence.

Before reading the story

Choose a time to read when you and the children are relaxed and have time to share the story.

Spend time looking at the illustrations and talk about what the book might be about before reading it together.

Encourage children to employ a phonics-first approach to tackling new words by sounding the words out.

After reading, talk about the book with the children:

- Ask the children why Hippo thought he would be able to ride a bike easily. Have the children had similar expectations when graduating from a trike, a balance bike or a bike with stabilisers to a big bike? Invite the children to share their experiences.

- Do the children agree with Aunty Hippo that it takes lots of practice to learn to ride a bike?

- Ask the children why it is important to wear a helmet when riding a bike.

Remind the children to listen carefully while others speak and to wait for their turn.

- Take the opportunity to open up a discussion on other skills the children may have found hard to learn. How did they learn their new skills? Did they take a lot of practice and patience?

- Ask the children to draw a picture of something they had to practise to learn. Ask them to write a sentence about their picture. At the end of the session, invite children to show their work to the others and to talk about what they have drawn.

29

For Isabelle, William A, William G, George, Max, Emily,

Leo, Caspar, Felix, Tabitha, Phoebe, Harry and Libby –S.G.

Franklin Watts
First published in 2023 by
Hodder and Stoughton

Text © Hodder and Stoughton Ltd, 2023
Illustrations © Trevor Dunton 2023

The right of Trevor Dunton to be identified as the illustrator
of this Work has been asserted in accordance with the
Copyright, Designs and Patents Act, 1988.

Editor: Jackie Hamley
Designer: Cathryn Gilbert

A CIP catalogue record for this book is available
from the British Library.

ISBN 978 1 4451 8206 3 (hardback)
ISBN 978 1 4451 8207 0 (paperback)
ISBN 978 1 4451 8832 4 (ebook)

Printed in China

Franklin Watts
An imprint of
Hachette Children's Books,
Part of Hodder and Stoughton
Carmelite House
50 Victoria Embankment
London EC4Y 0DZ

An Hachette UK company
www.hachettechildrens.co.uk